Moo and Moo
and the Little Calf too

STORY BY Jane Millton

ILLUSTRATED BY Deborah Hinde

ALLEN&UNWIN

SYDNEY · MELBOURNE · AUCKLAND · LONDON

High on a hill overlooking the sea,
In the long green grass by the tōtara tree,
Moo and Moo and the little calf too
Were sleeping together as all cows do.

All was quiet on the seafront hill.
The night was clear and the air was still.
The stars were out, the moon up high
In a bright and luminous midnight sky.

Then all of a sudden, with a jolt and a lift,
The grass on the top began to shift.
The sleeping cows were now wide awake,
As the Clarence Valley began to SHAKE!

With a bump and a shudder
And a wobble of the udder,
With a rocking and a rolling
And a slip and a slide,
Moo and Moo and the little calf too
Began . . . their . . . ride.

"Hold on, Moo!" mooed Moo to Moo.
They stayed together with the little calf too.
"We'll be all right! This might even be fun . . .
It's something that we've never, ever, ever done."

They braced and they swayed,
And they stood quite still,
All together as the earth began its pull.
"Off we go in the bright super moon!
But I'm sure we'll stop very, very soon."

On and on, past the trough and the tank,
Past the tōtara and the tussock
And their favourite grassy bank.
Then down,
     down,
          down
               with a rumble and a roar,
Until their ride ended at the valley floor.

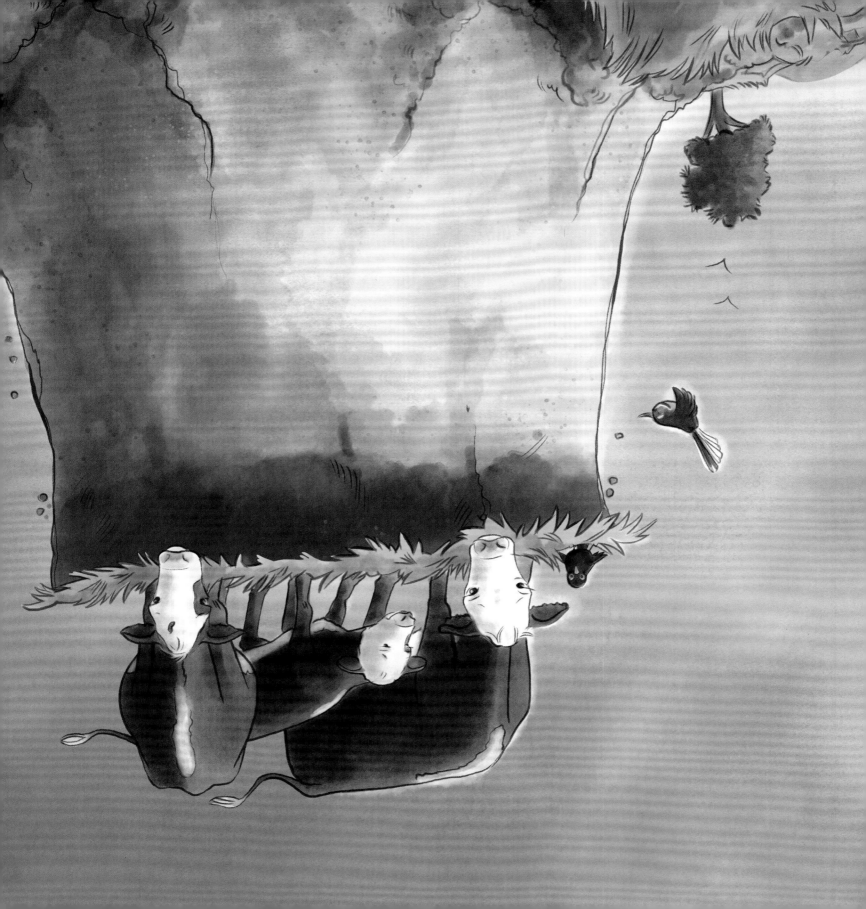

The sun came up – that moon had gone.
The birds were awake and were singing their song.
The cows looked around and saw they were stranded
On a grassy little platform, just where it had landed.

"Oh, what a sight!" mooed Moo to Moo.
It all looked so different as they gazed at the view.
Had the seabed lifted?
Or had the coastline drifted?

Moo and Moo and the little calf too
Began to wonder what to do.
"Shall we jump, or shall we stay?
Maybe there's help, and it's on the way?"

Then a helicopter appeared and flew around!
A beating, thudding, whirring and very noisy sound.
Around and around, the helicopter flew.
"I wonder if it's Richie?" mooed Moo to Moo.

Oh, how exciting! In the distance they saw
Some people were coming – two and then four.
With picks and shovels, they came closer to the spot
To save those stranded cows, believe it or not!

"Hello there, girls!" said the men with a shout.
"We've all come to help you and get you out.
We've missed you so much and we want you home.
We will keep you safe and you'll never be alone."

With the picks and the shovels, the men began to hack.
Then Moo followed Moo down the narrow limestone track.
On through the ruptures, and on through the rubble,
The cows crossed safely without any trouble.

How happy they were to be saved by the men:
Willie and Julian, Tony and Ben.
Gently and slowly the cows got to the gates,
And who should be there but their Hereford mates.

They skipped and they kicked their legs in the air,
As they ran down the hill without a care!

They got to the paddock, and had a drink and a rest,
And they all agreed that this place was the best.

What a night to remember,
The fourteenth of November!

About this story

This story is based on the real-life adventure of two Hereford cows and a calf from the Clarence Valley in Marlborough.

On Monday 14 November 2016, at two minutes after midnight, there was a big earthquake in the South Island of New Zealand, not far from the town of Kaikōura. It caused a lot of damage to people's homes and businesses – and it also destroyed the hillside these cows had been sleeping on! The three brave cows quickly became famous, as people all over the world shared an amazing image of them stranded on an "island" of grass. The cows were soon rescued. They live at Waipapa, a farm in the Clarence Valley owned by the Millton family.

Did you know?

- Earthquakes are measured using the Richter scale, and the Kaikōura earthquake was 7.8 – that's really big!

- The Kaikōura earthquake was so powerful that it lifted the seabed 5.5 metres out of the water in some places. That's even higher than a two-storey house!

- The island that the cows were stranded on moved 80 metres from its starting point. The earth was jumping around so much that the cows had to "surf" on the island to keep their balance!

For Kate, Paddy, Charlotte, Ted and George,
and for Moo and Moo and the little calf too. J.M.

For M., who ensured I was well fed and watered
while I was in my studio. Moo! D.H.

First published in 2017

Text copyright © Jane Millton 2017
Illustrations copyright © Deborah Hinde 2017

Allen & Unwin
Level 3, 228 Queen Street
Auckland 1010, New Zealand
Phone: (64 9) 377 3800
Email: info@allenandunwin.com
Web: www.allenandunwin.co.nz

Allen & Unwin
83 Alexander Street
Crows Nest NSW 2065, Australia
Phone: (61 2) 8425 0100

A catalogue record for this book is available
from the National Library of New Zealand

ISBN 978 1 877505 92 8

Design by Kate Barraclough
Set in 17/23 pt Founders Caslon

Printed in China by C&C Offset Printing Co. Ltd

10 9 8 7 6 5 4